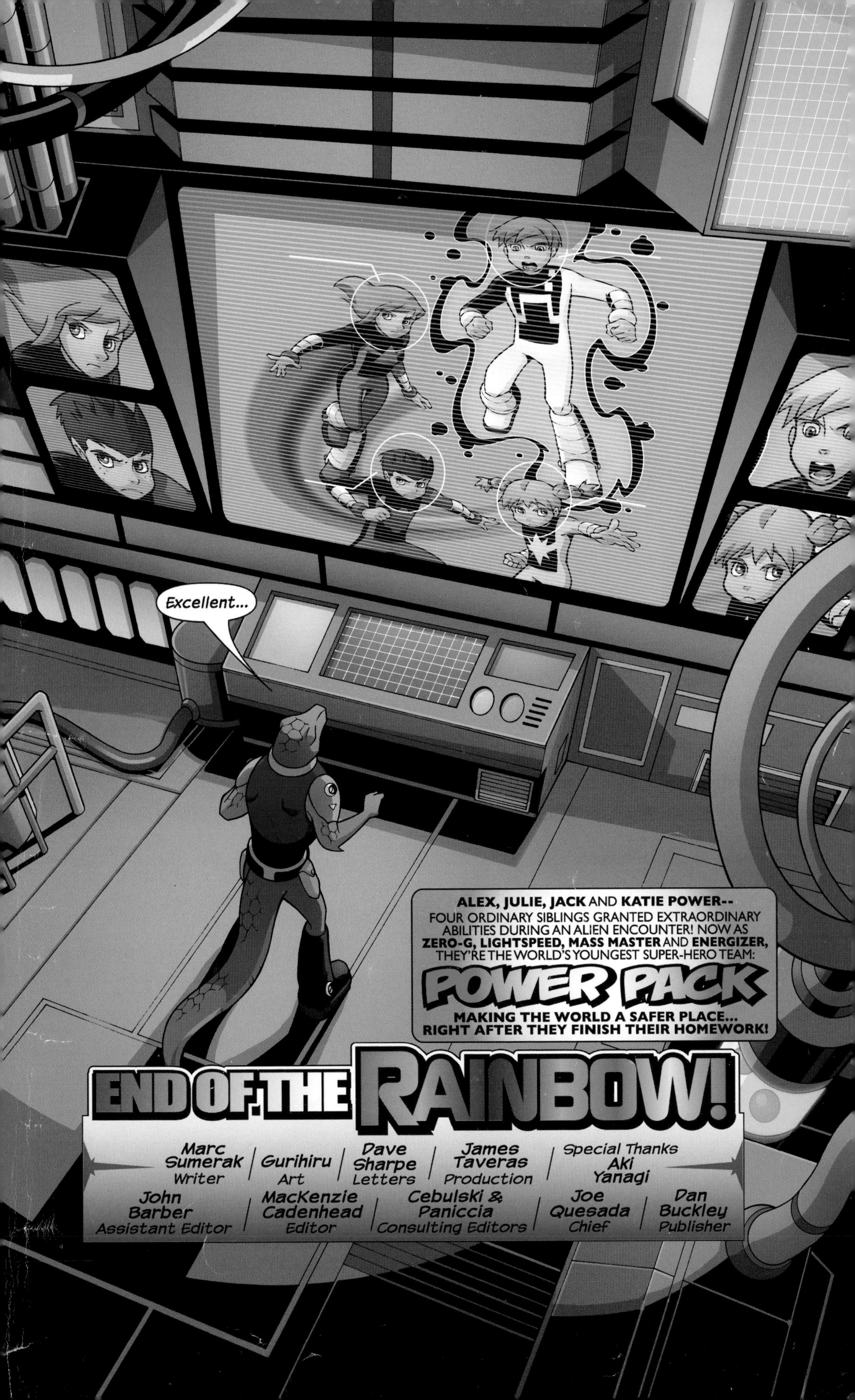

Excellent...
ALEX, JULIE, JACK AND KATIE POWER-- FOUR ORDINARY SIBLINGS GRANTED EXTRAORDINARY ABILITIES DURING AN ALIEN ENCOUNTER! NOW AS ZERO-G, LIGHTSPEED, MASS MASTER AND ENERGIZER, THEY'RE THE WORLD'S YOUNGEST SUPER-HERO TEAM:
POWER PACK
MAKING THE WORLD A SAFER PLACE... RIGHT AFTER THEY FINISH THEIR HOMEWORK!
END OF THE RAINBOW!
Marc Sumerak Writer
Gurihiru Art
Dave Sharpe Letters
James Taveras Production
Special Thanks Aki Yanagi
John Barber Assistant Editor
MacKenzie Cadenhead Editor
Cebulski & Paniccia Consulting Editors
Joe Quesada Chief
Dan Buckley Publisher

VISIT US AT
www.abdopub.com

Spotlight, a division of ABDO Publishing Company Inc., is the school and library distributor of the Marvel Entertainment books.

Library bound edition © 2006

Library of Congress Cataloging-in-Publication Data

End of the Rainbow!

ISBN 1-59961-032-9 (Reinforced Library Bound Edition)

All Spotlight books are reinforced library binding and manufactured in the United States of America

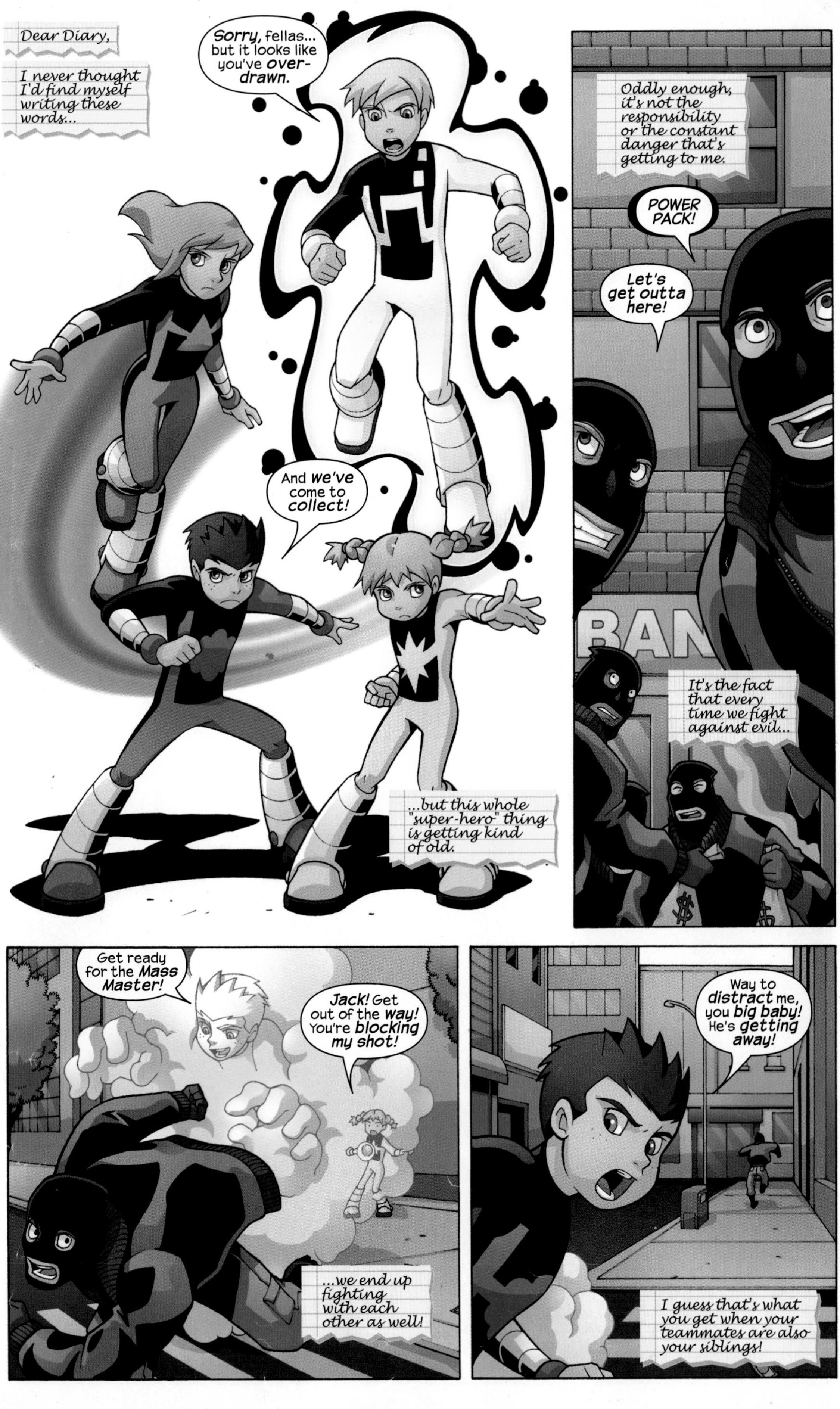
Dear Diary,
I never thought I'd find myself writing these words...
Sorry, fellas... but it looks like you've over-drawn.
And we've come to collect!
...but this whole "super-hero" thing is getting kind of old.
Oddly enough, it's not the responsibility or the constant danger that's getting to me.
POWER PACK!
Let's get outta here!
BAN
It's the fact that every time we fight against evil...
Get ready for the Mass Master!
Jack! Get out of the way! You're blocking my shot!
...we end up fighting with each other as well!
Way to distract me, you big baby! He's getting away!
I guess that's what you get when your teammates are also your siblings!

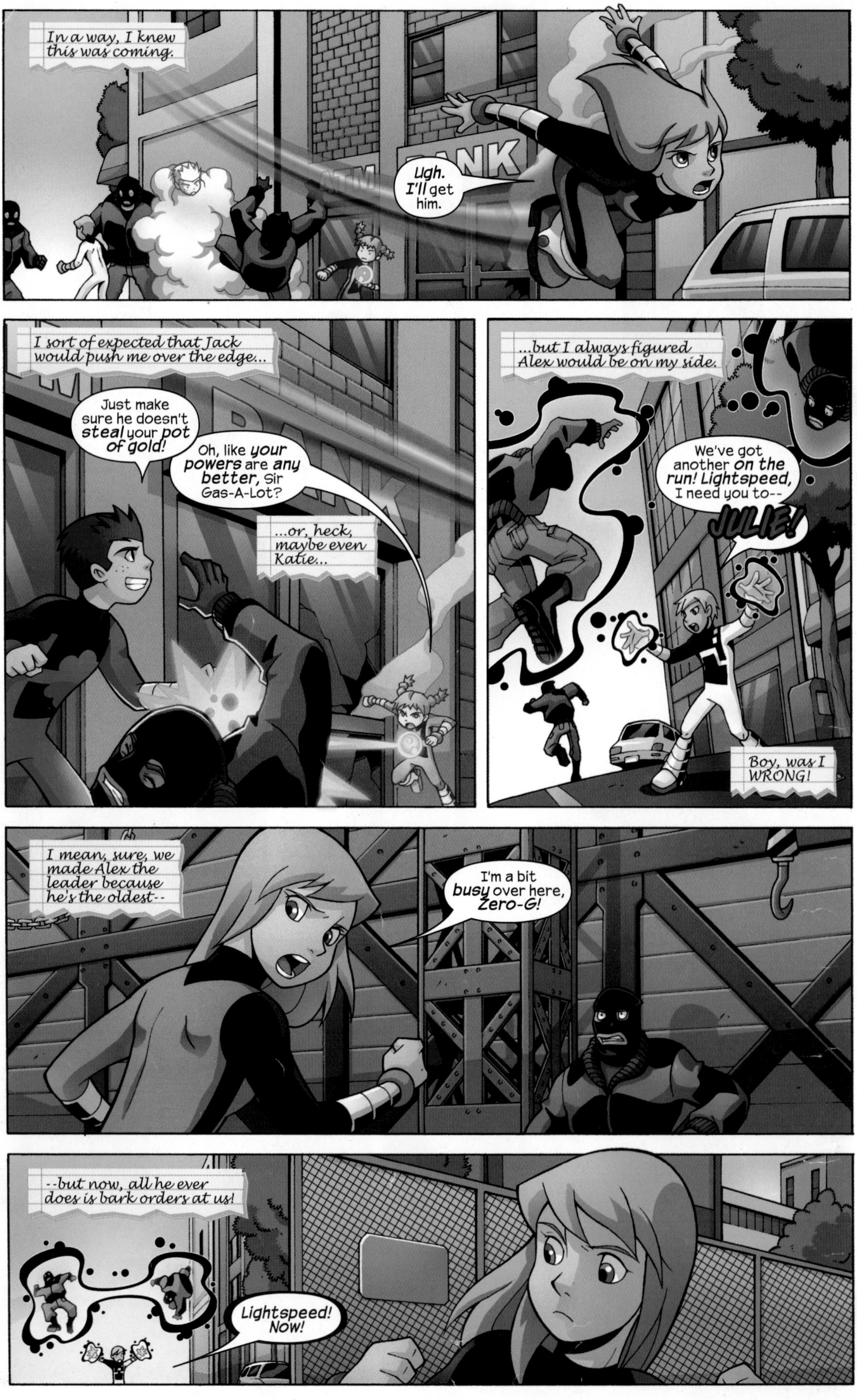
In a way, I knew this was coming.
BANK
ATM
Ugh. I'll get him.
I sort of expected that Jack would push me over the edge...
Just make sure he doesn't steal your pot of gold!
Oh, like your powers are any better, Sir Gas-A-Lot?
...or, heck, maybe even Katie...
...but I always figured Alex would be on my side.
We've got another on the run! Lightspeed, I need you to--
JULIE!
Boy, was I WRONG!
I mean, sure, we made Alex the leader because he's the oldest--
I'm a bit busy over here, Zero-G!
--but now, all he ever does is bark orders at us!
Lightspeed! NOW!

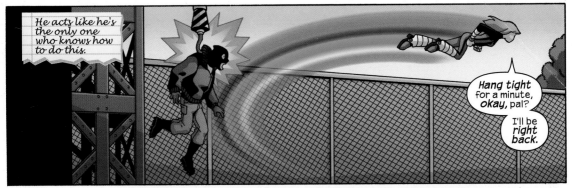

He acts like he's the only one who knows how to do this.

Hang tight for a minute, *okay*, pal? I'll be *right* back.

Like my ideas are never good enough.

Julie! He's--

Yeah, yeah... I heard you the *first time*...

Well, I'm tired of doing all the hard work and still feeling like I don't count!

Gotcha!

Hey! Lemme go!

It may not bother little kids like Jack and Katie...

There. That takes care of *him*. Now to *deal* with--

...but it's just not working for me anymore.

No! He's gone!

That's why I've come to an important decision...

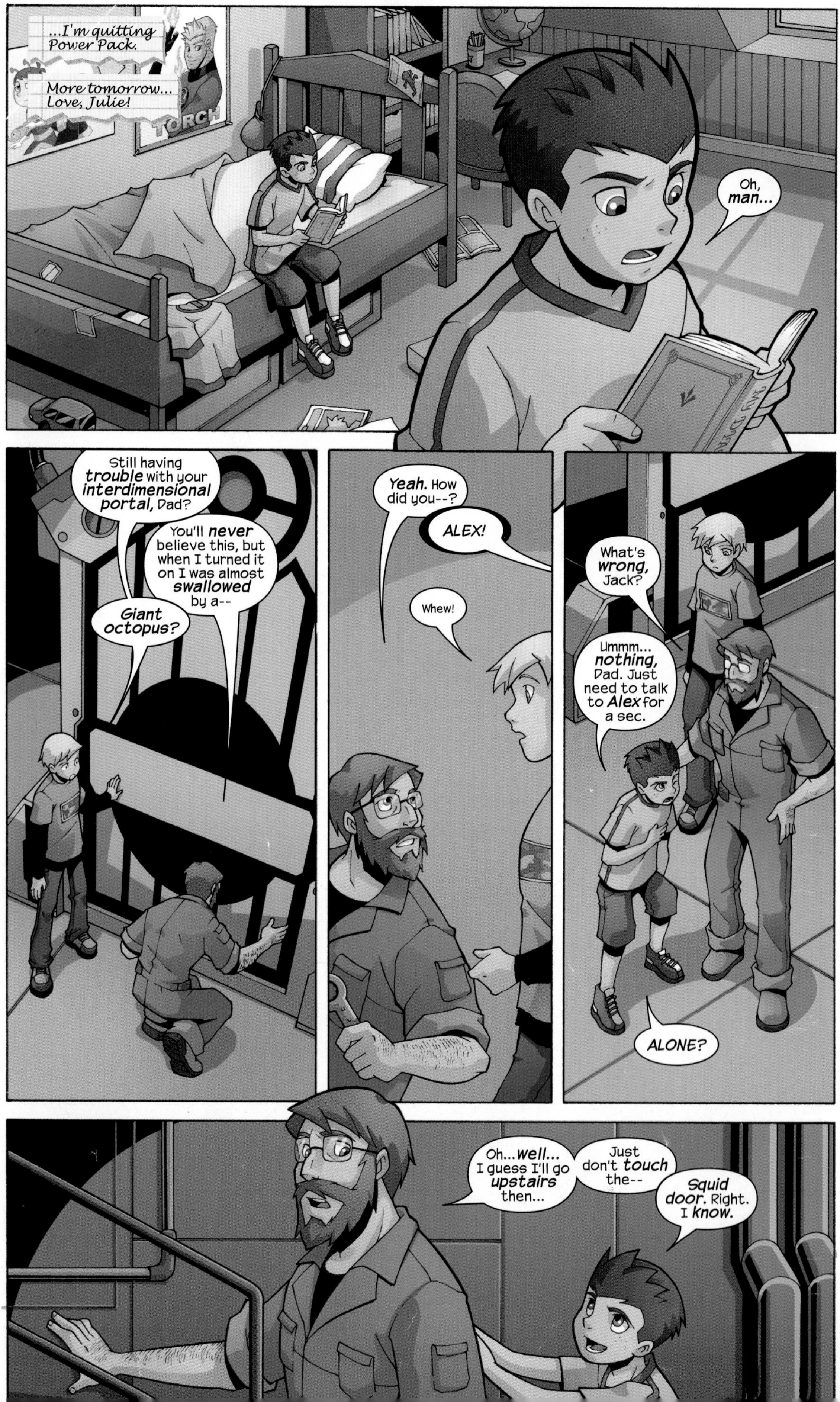

...I'm quitting Power Pack.
More tomorrow... Love, Julie!
TORCH
Oh, man...
Still having trouble with your interdimensional portal, Dad?
You'll never believe this, but when I turned it on I was almost swallowed by a--
Giant octopus?
Yeah. How did you--?
ALEX!
Whew!
What's wrong, Jack?
Ummm... nothing, Dad. Just need to talk to Alex for a sec.
ALONE?
Oh...well... I guess I'll go upstairs then...
Just don't touch the--
Squid door. Right. I know.

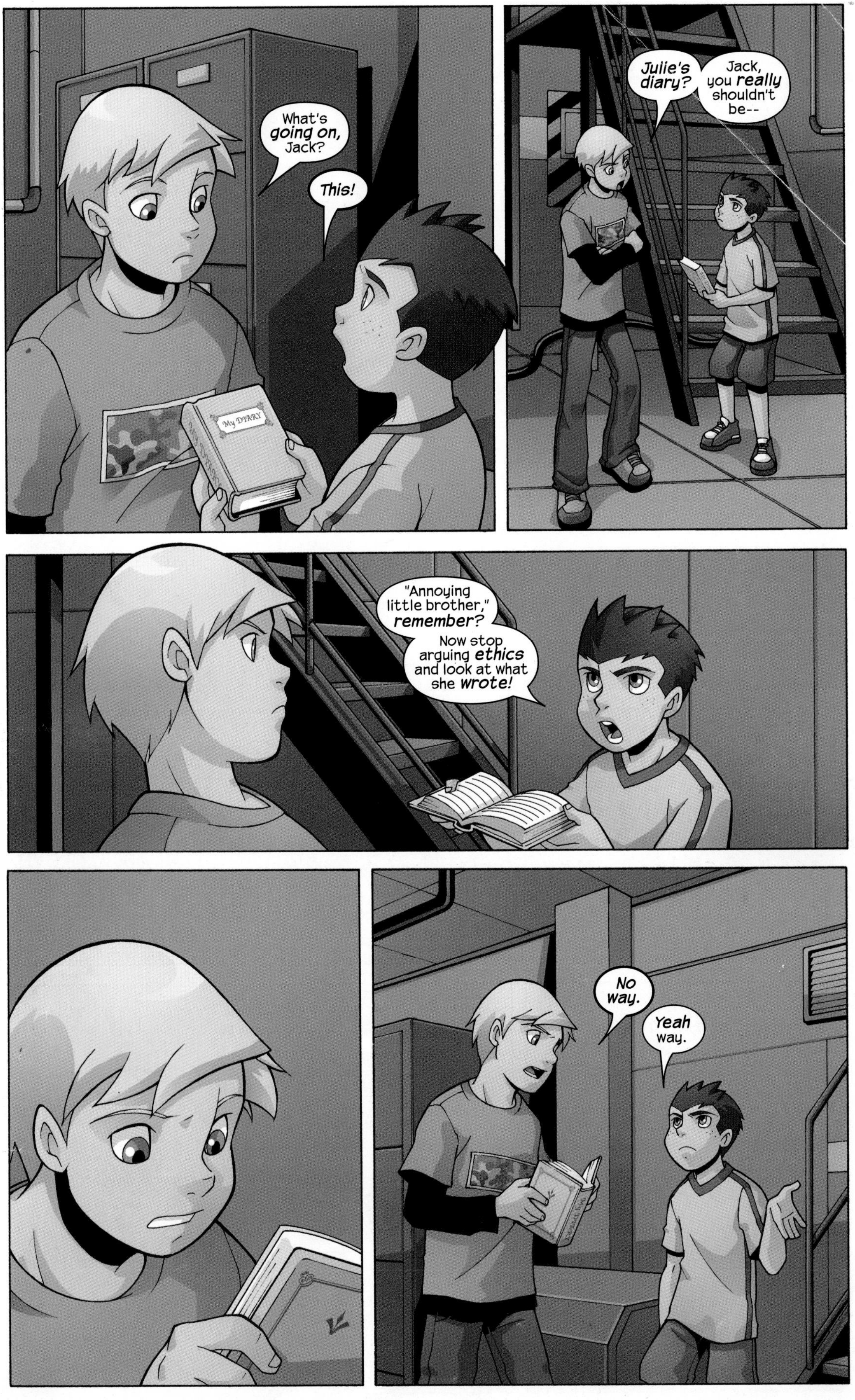

What's going on, Jack?
This!
Julie's diary?
Jack, you really shouldn't be--
My DIARY
"Annoying little brother," remember?
Now stop arguing ethics and look at what she wrote!
No way.
Yeah way.

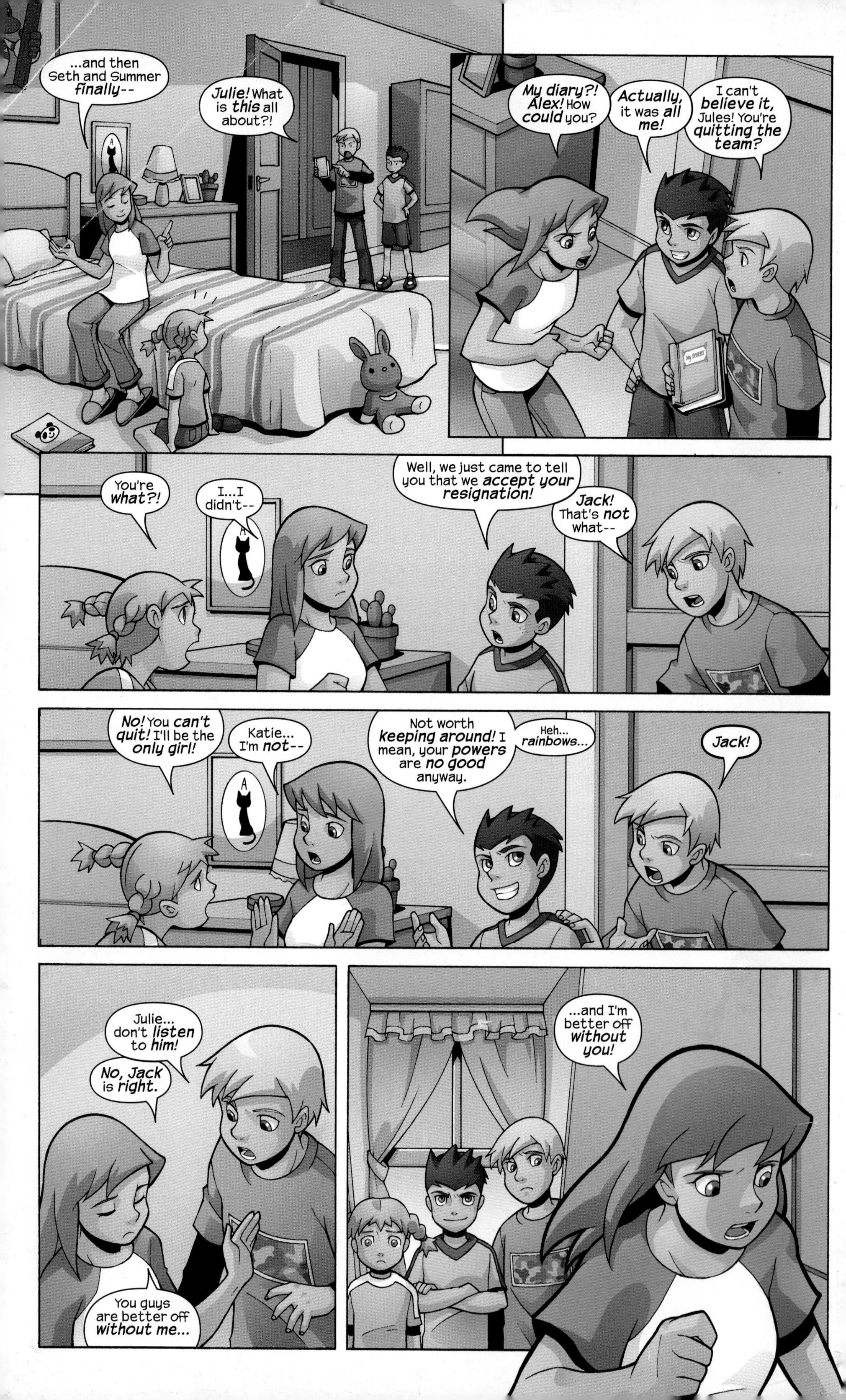
...and then Seth and Summer *finally*--
Julie! What is *this* all about?!
My diary?! Alex! How *could* you?
Actually, it was *all me!*
I can't *believe it,* Jules! You're *quitting the team?*
You're *what?!*
I...I didn't--
Well, we just came to tell you that we *accept your resignation!*
Jack! That's *not* what--
No! You *can't quit!* I'll be the *only girl!*
Katie... I'm *not*--
Not worth *keeping around!* I mean, your *powers* are *no good* anyway.
Heh... *rainbows...*
Jack!
Julie... don't *listen* to *him!*
No, Jack is *right.*
You guys are better off *without me...*
...and I'm better off *without you!*

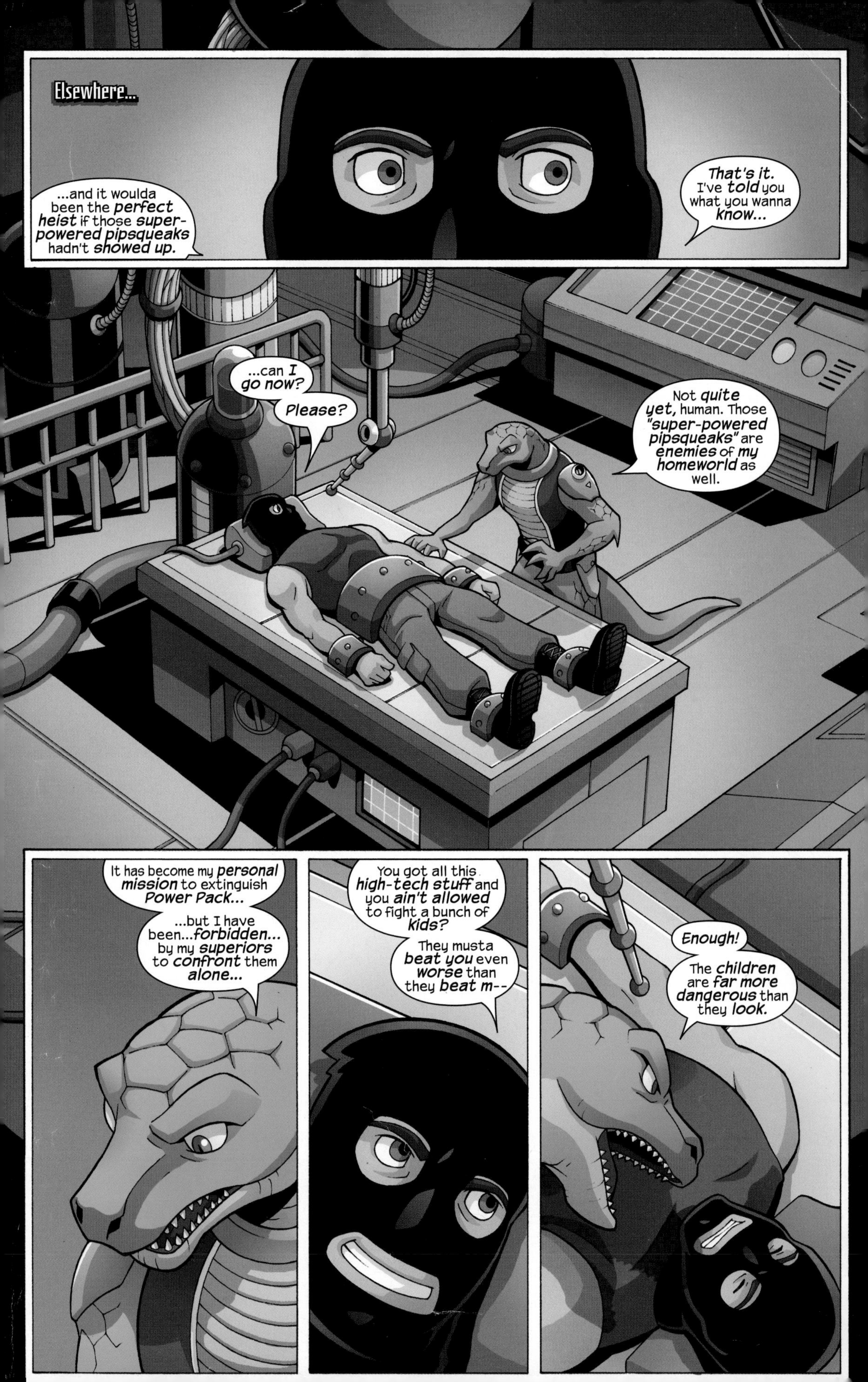
Elsewhere...
...and it woulda been the perfect heist if those super-powered pipsqueaks hadn't showed up.
That's it. I've told you what you wanna know...
...can I go now?
Please?
Not quite yet, human. Those "super-powered pipsqueaks" are enemies of my homeworld as well.
It has become my personal mission to extinguish Power Pack...
...but I have been...forbidden... by my superiors to confront them alone...
You got all this high-tech stuff and you ain't allowed to fight a bunch of kids?
They musta beat you even worse than they beat m--
Enough!
The children are far more dangerous than they look.

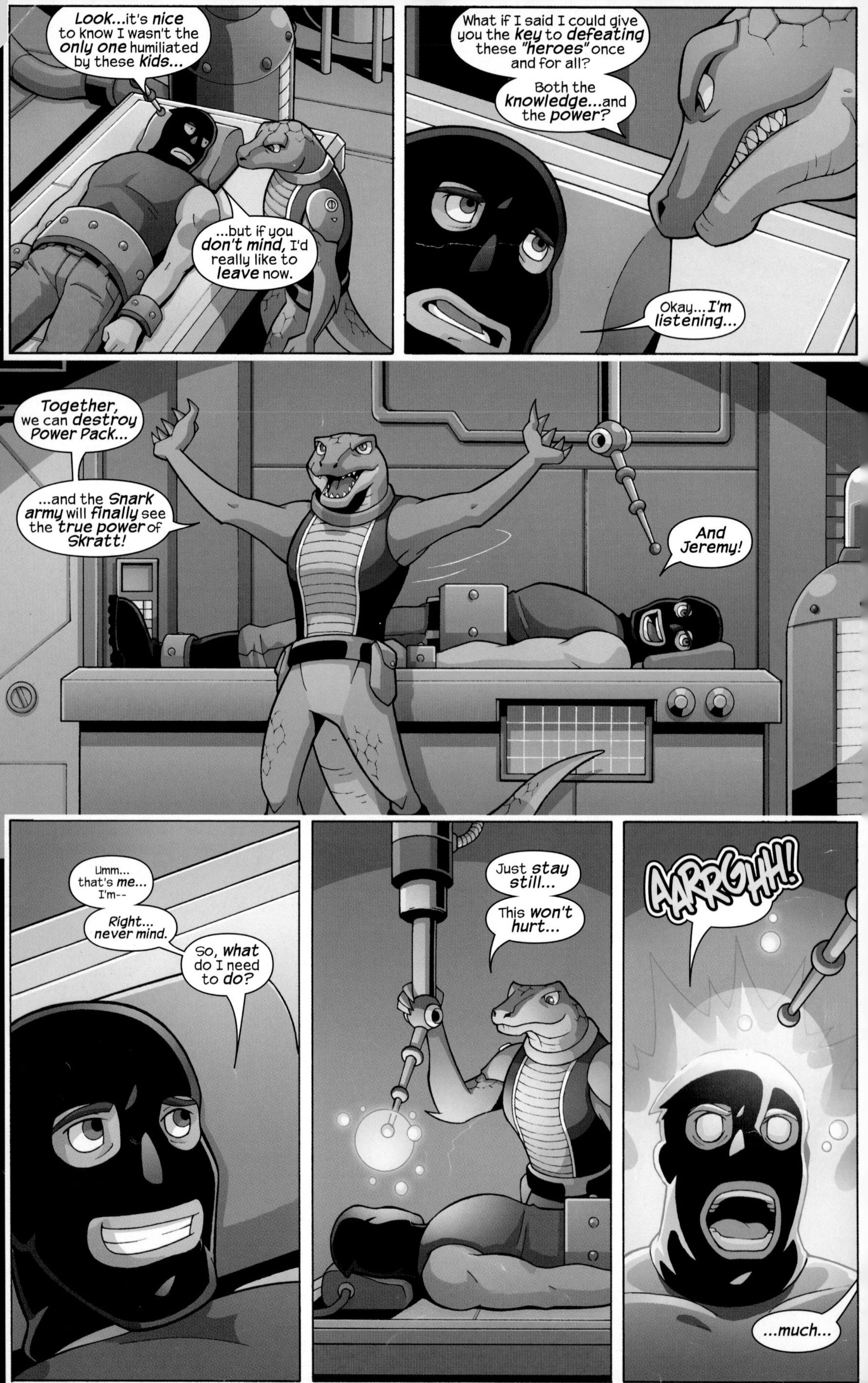
Look...it's nice to know I wasn't the only one humiliated by these kids...
...but if you don't mind, I'd really like to leave now.
What if I said I could give you the key to defeating these "heroes" once and for all?
Both the knowledge...and the power?
Okay...I'm listening...
Together, we can destroy Power Pack...
...and the Snark army will finally see the true power of Skratt!
And Jeremy!
Umm... that's me... I'm--
Right... never mind.
So, what do I need to do?
Just stay still...
This won't hurt...
AARRGHH!
...much...

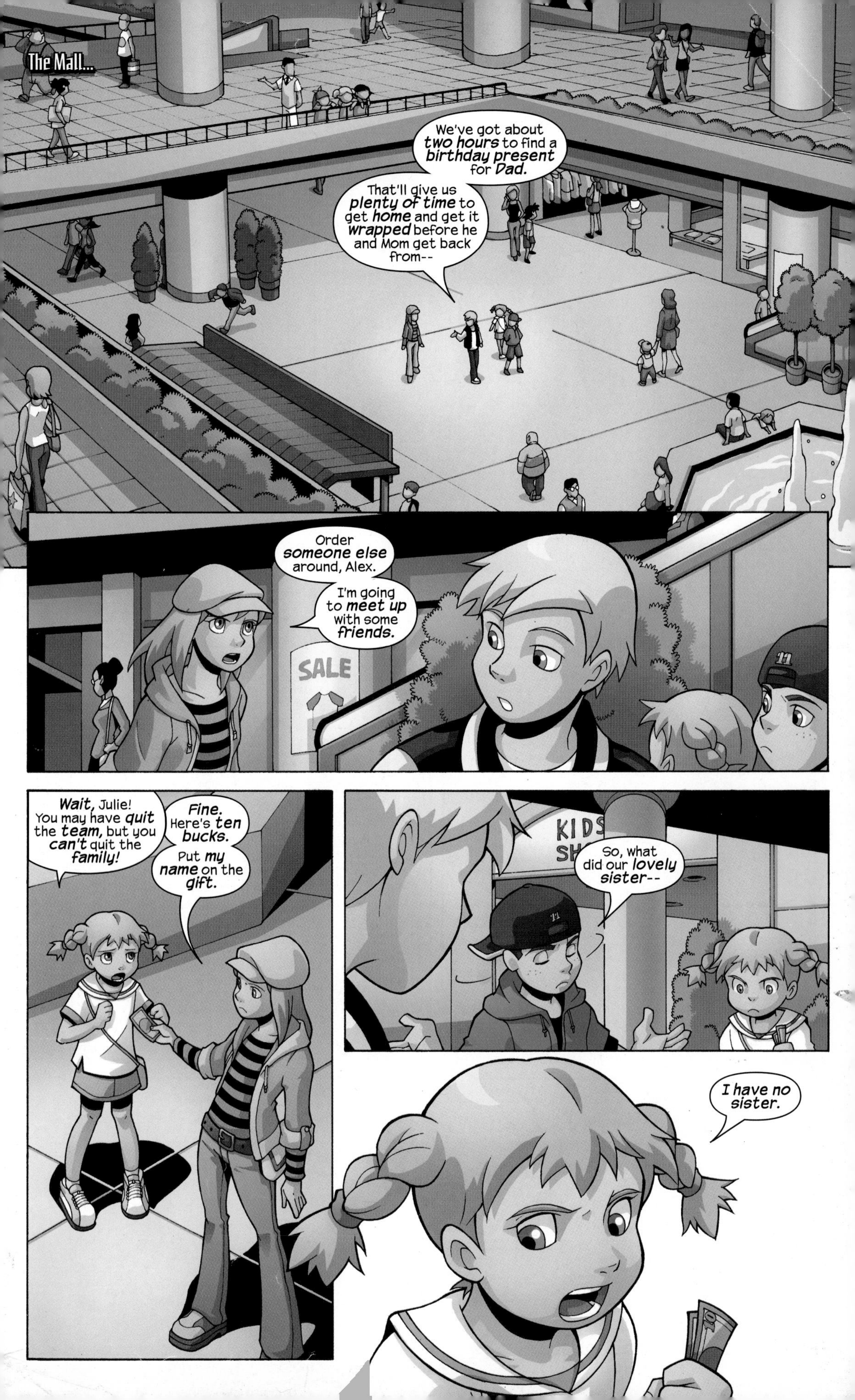
The Mall...
We've got about two hours to find a birthday present for Dad.
That'll give us plenty of time to get home and get it wrapped before he and Mom get back from--
Order someone else around, Alex.
I'm going to meet up with some friends.
SALE
Wait, Julie! You may have quit the team, but you can't quit the family!
Fine. Here's ten bucks.
Put my name on the gift.
So, what did our lovely sister--
I have no sister.

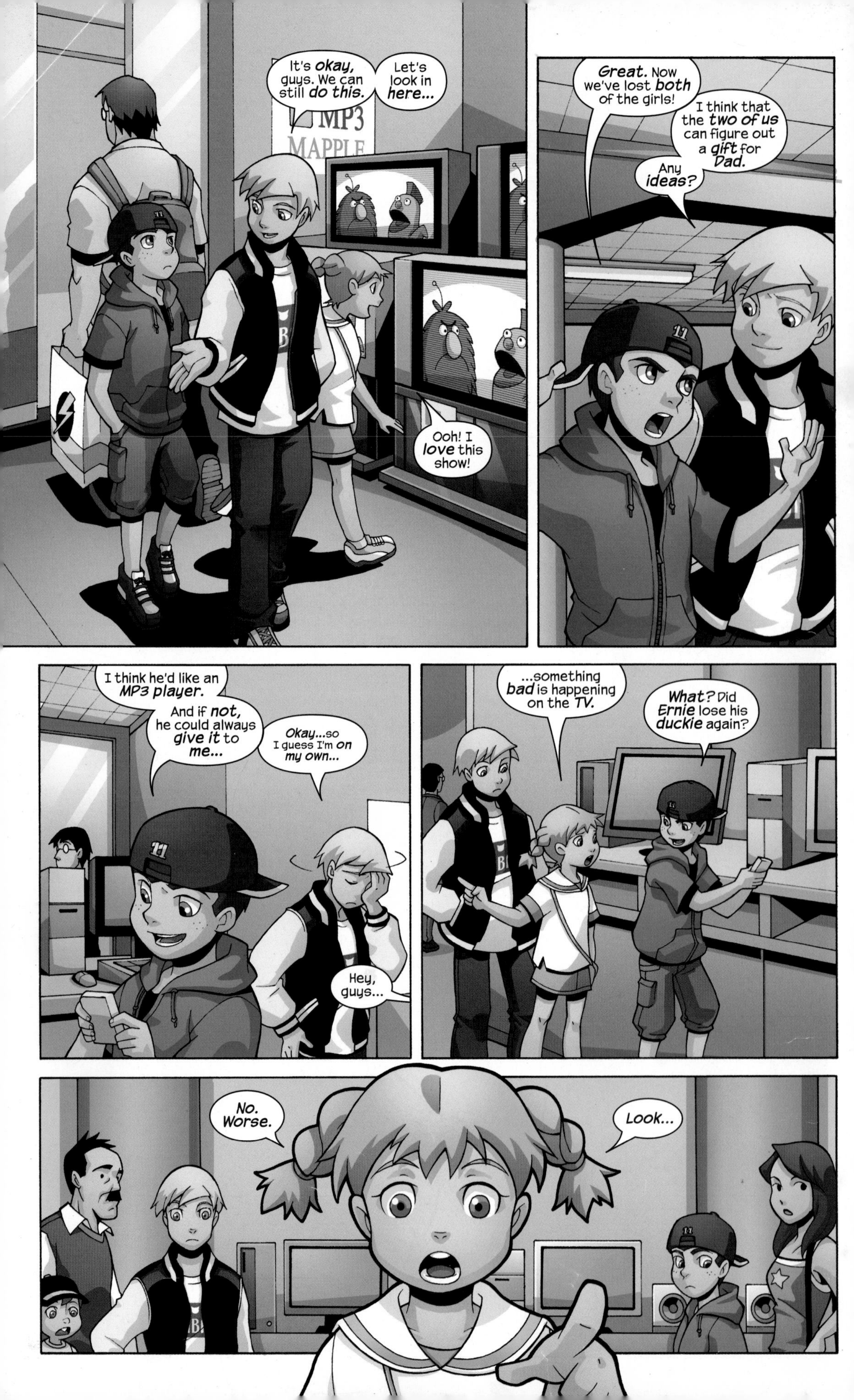

It's okay, guys. We can still do this.
Let's look in here...
MP3
MAPPLE
Ooh! I love this show!
Great. Now we've lost both of the girls!
I think that the two of us can figure out a gift for Dad.
Any ideas?
I think he'd like an MP3 player.
And if not, he could always give it to me...
Okay...so I guess I'm on my own...
Hey, guys...
...something bad is happening on the TV.
What? Did Ernie lose his duckie again?
No. Worse.
Look...

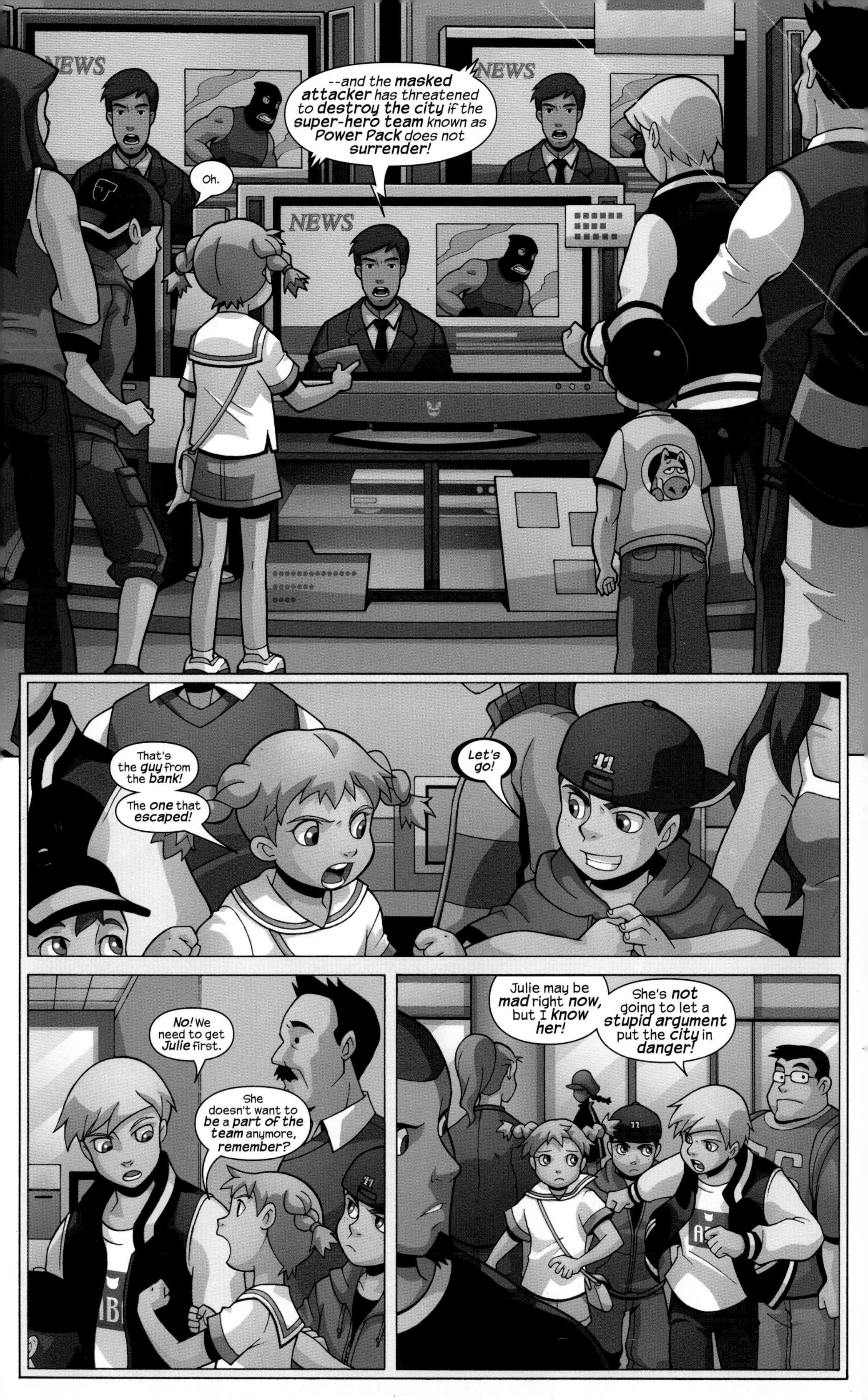
NEWS
--and the masked attacker has threatened to destroy the city if the super-hero team known as Power Pack does not surrender!
Oh.
That's the guy from the bank!
The one that escaped!
Let's go!
No! We need to get Julie first.
She doesn't want to be a part of the team anymore, remember?
Julie may be mad right now, but I know her!
She's not going to let a stupid argument put the city in danger!

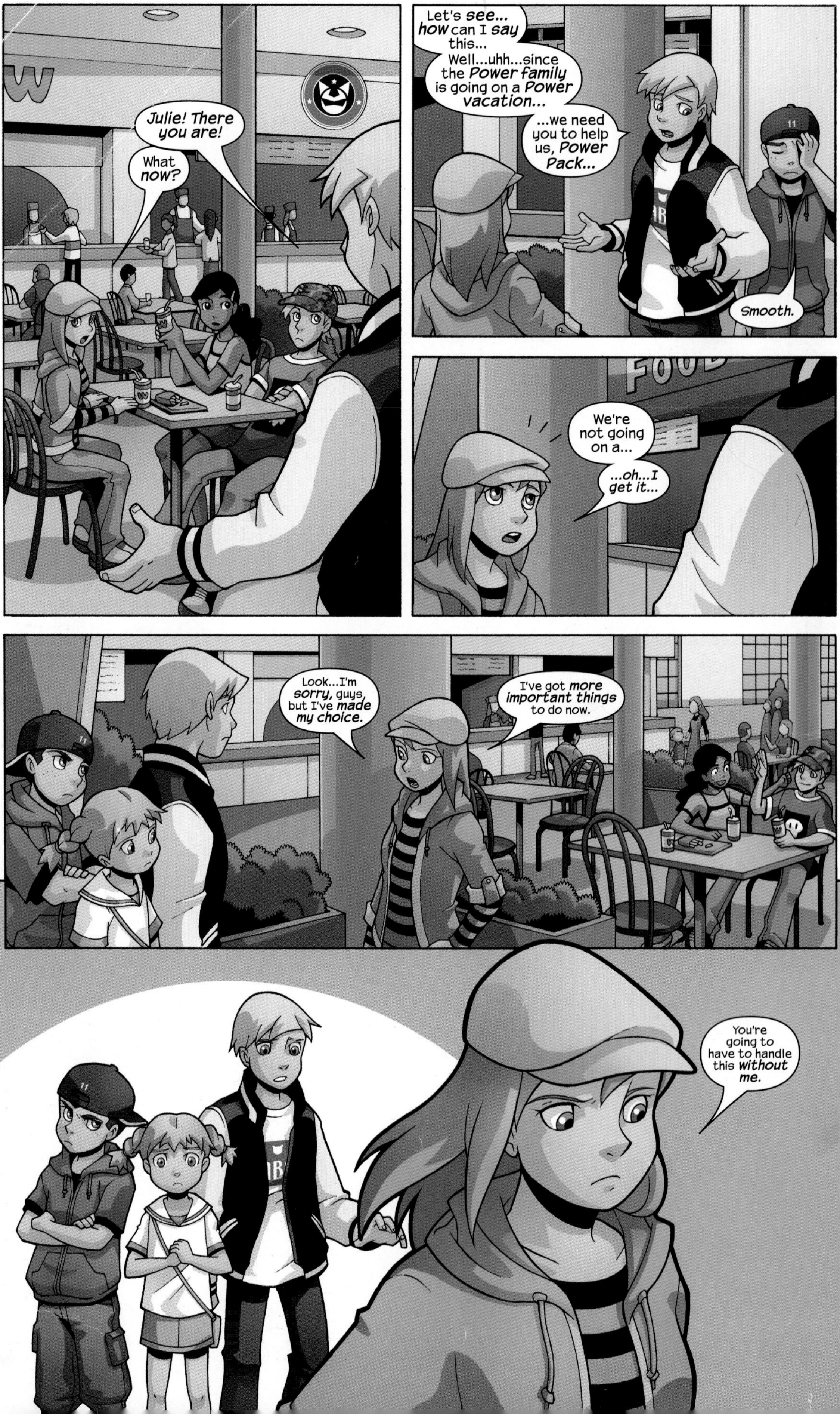

Julie! There you are!
What now?
Let's see... how can I say this...
Well...uhh...since the Power family is going on a Power vacation...
...we need you to help us, Power Pack...
Smooth.
We're not going on a...
...oh...I get it...
Look...I'm sorry, guys, but I've made my choice.
I've got more important things to do now.
You're going to have to handle this without me.

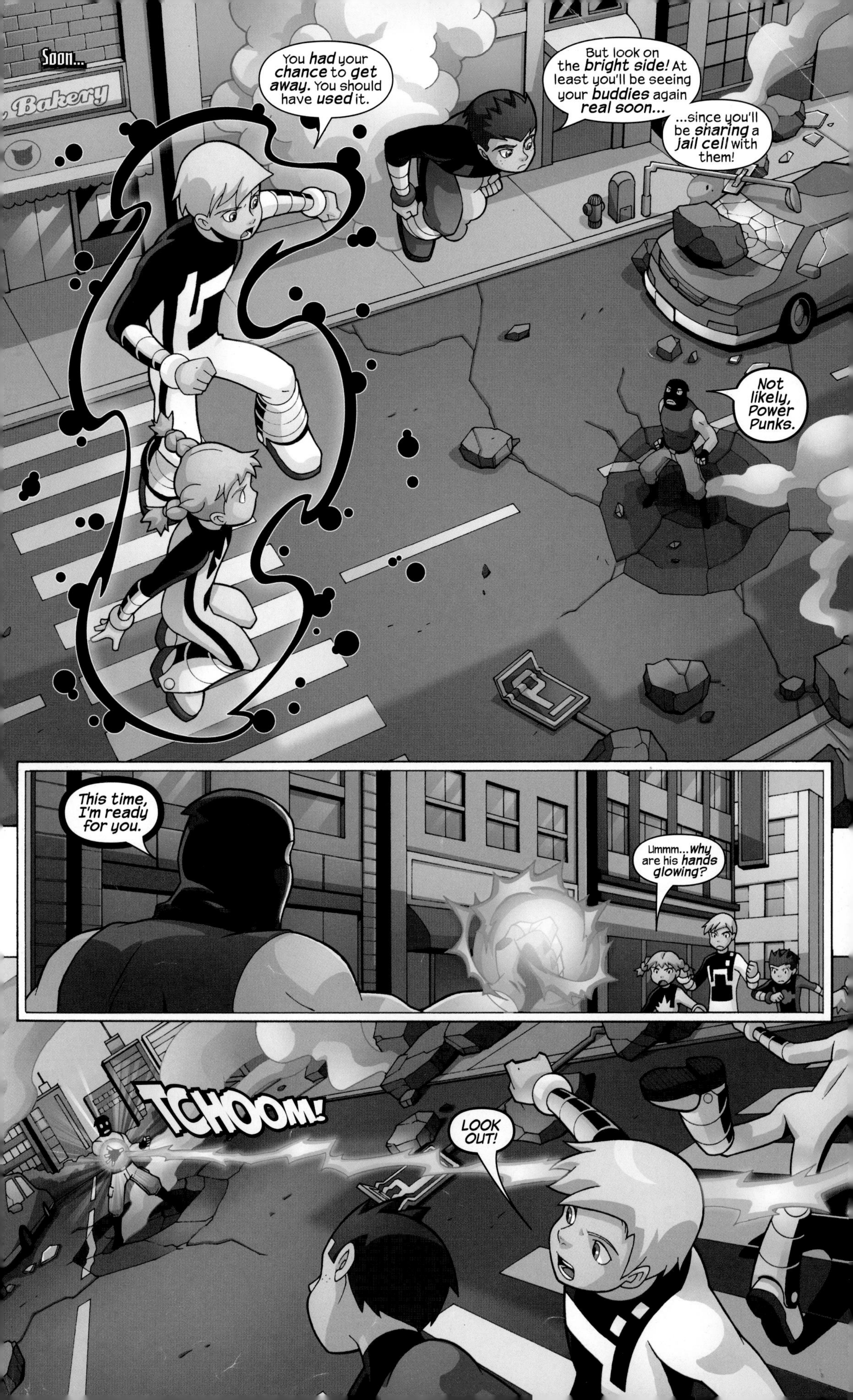
Soon...
You had your chance to get away. You should have used it.
But look on the bright side! At least you'll be seeing your buddies again real soon...
...since you'll be sharing a jail cell with them!
Not likely, Power Punks.
This time, I'm ready for you.
Ummm...why are his hands glowing?
TCHOOM!
LOOK OUT!

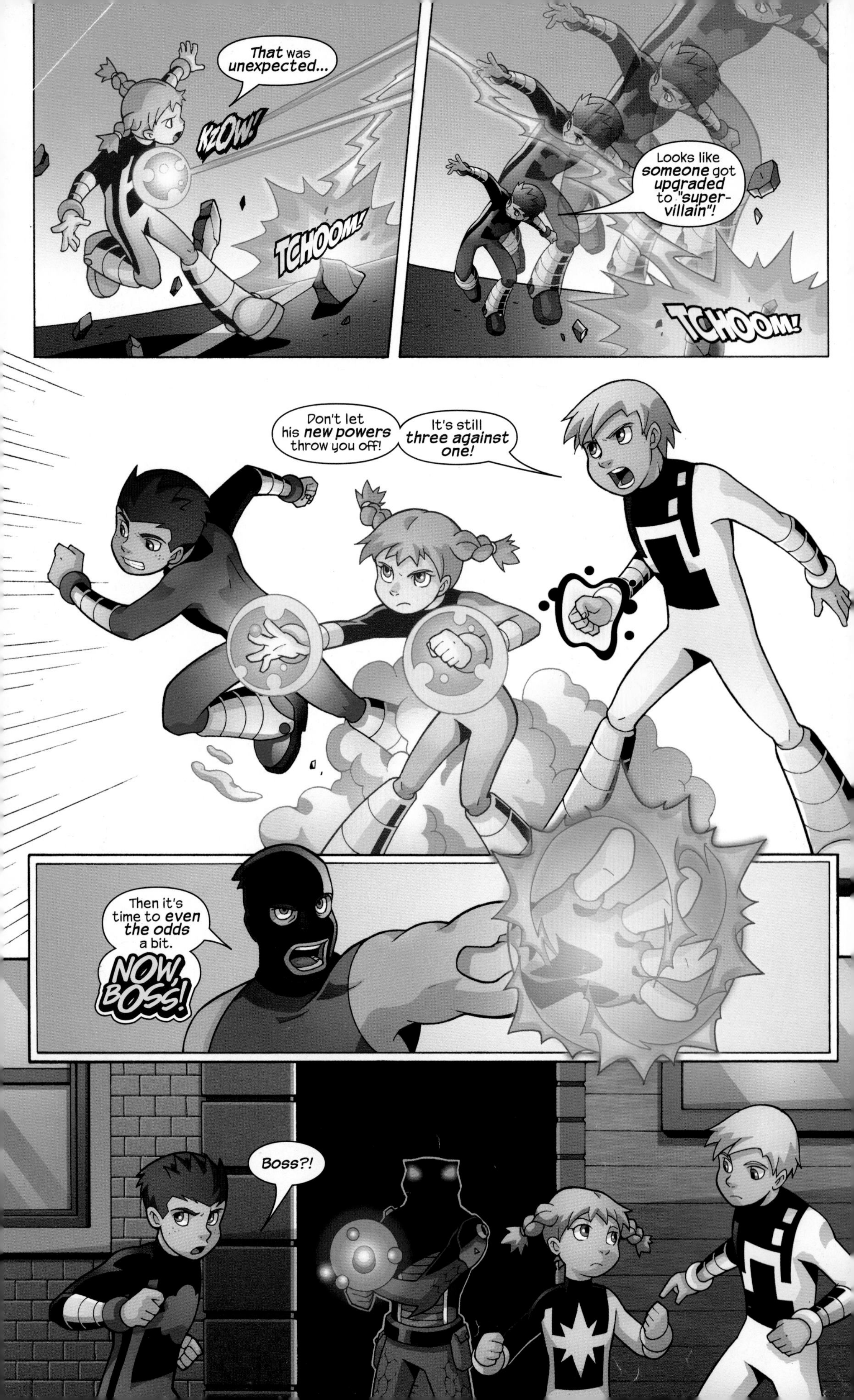
That was unexpected...
KZOW!
TCHOOM!
Looks like someone got upgraded to "super-villain"!
TCHOOM!
Don't let his new powers throw you off!
It's still three against one!
Then it's time to even the odds a bit.
NOW, BOSS!
Boss?!

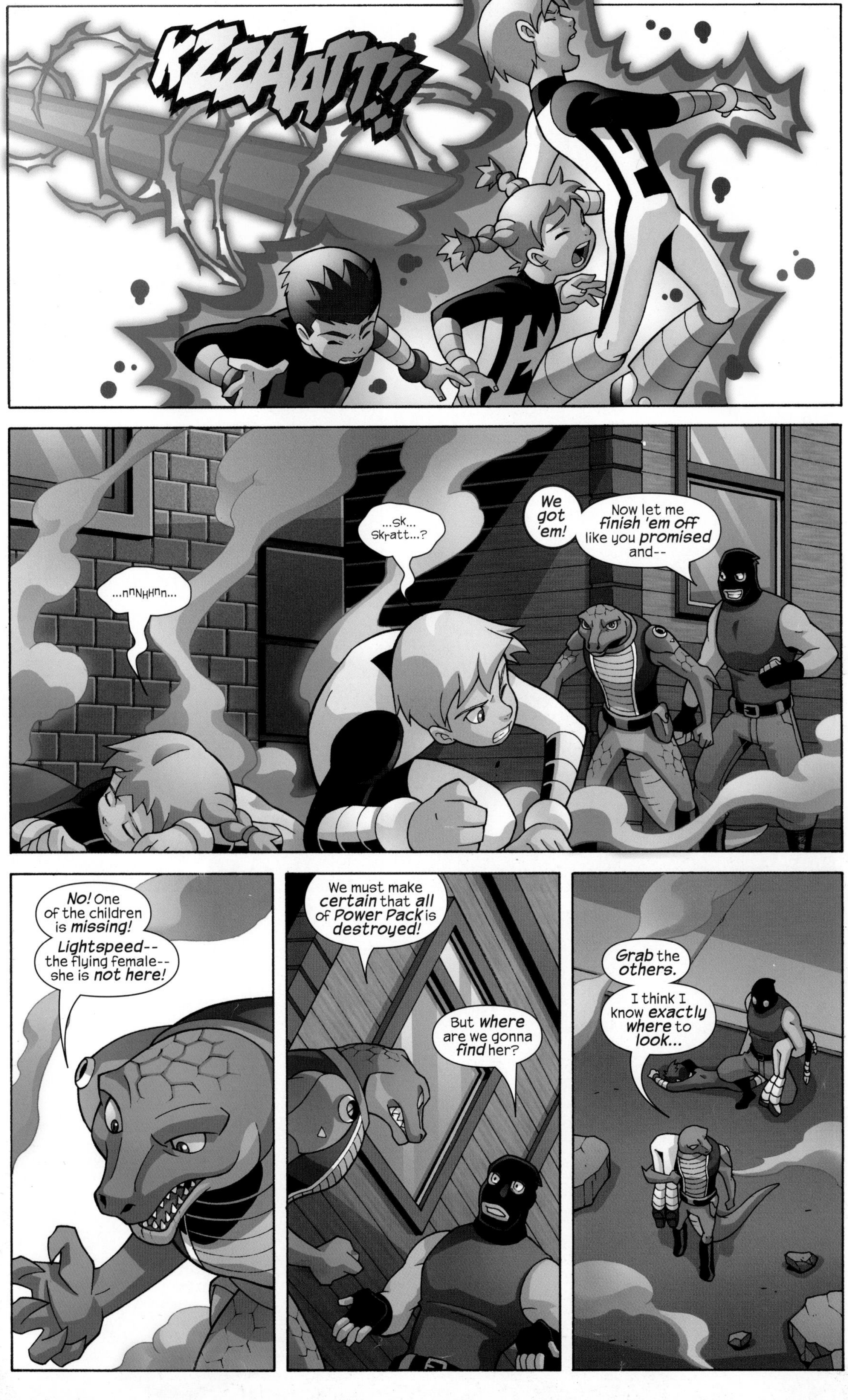
KZZAATT!!
...nnNHnn...
...sk...
Skratt...?
We got 'em!
Now let me finish 'em off like you promised and--
No! One of the children is missing!
Lightspeed-- the flying female-- she is not here!
We must make certain that all of Power Pack is destroyed!
But where are we gonna find her?
Grab the others.
I think I know exactly where to look...

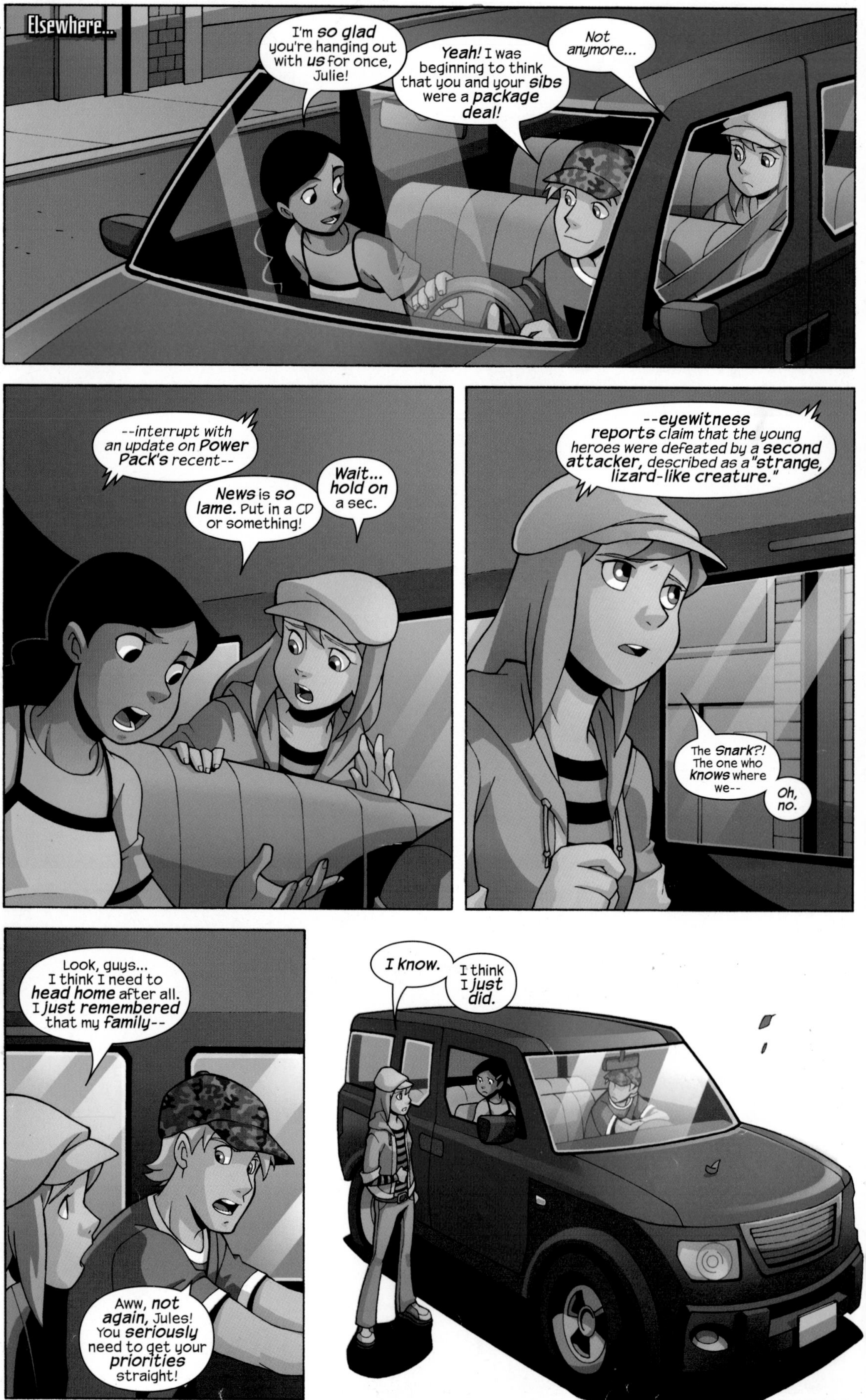

Elsewhere...
I'm so glad you're hanging out with us for once, Julie!
Yeah! I was beginning to think that you and your sibs were a package deal!
Not anymore...
--interrupt with an update on Power Pack's recent--
News is so lame. Put in a CD or something!
Wait... hold on a sec.
--eyewitness reports claim that the young heroes were defeated by a second attacker, described as a "strange, lizard-like creature."
The Snark?! The one who knows where we--
Oh, no.
Look, guys... I think I need to head home after all. I just remembered that my family--
Aww, not again, Jules! You seriously need to get your priorities straight!
I know.
I think I just did.

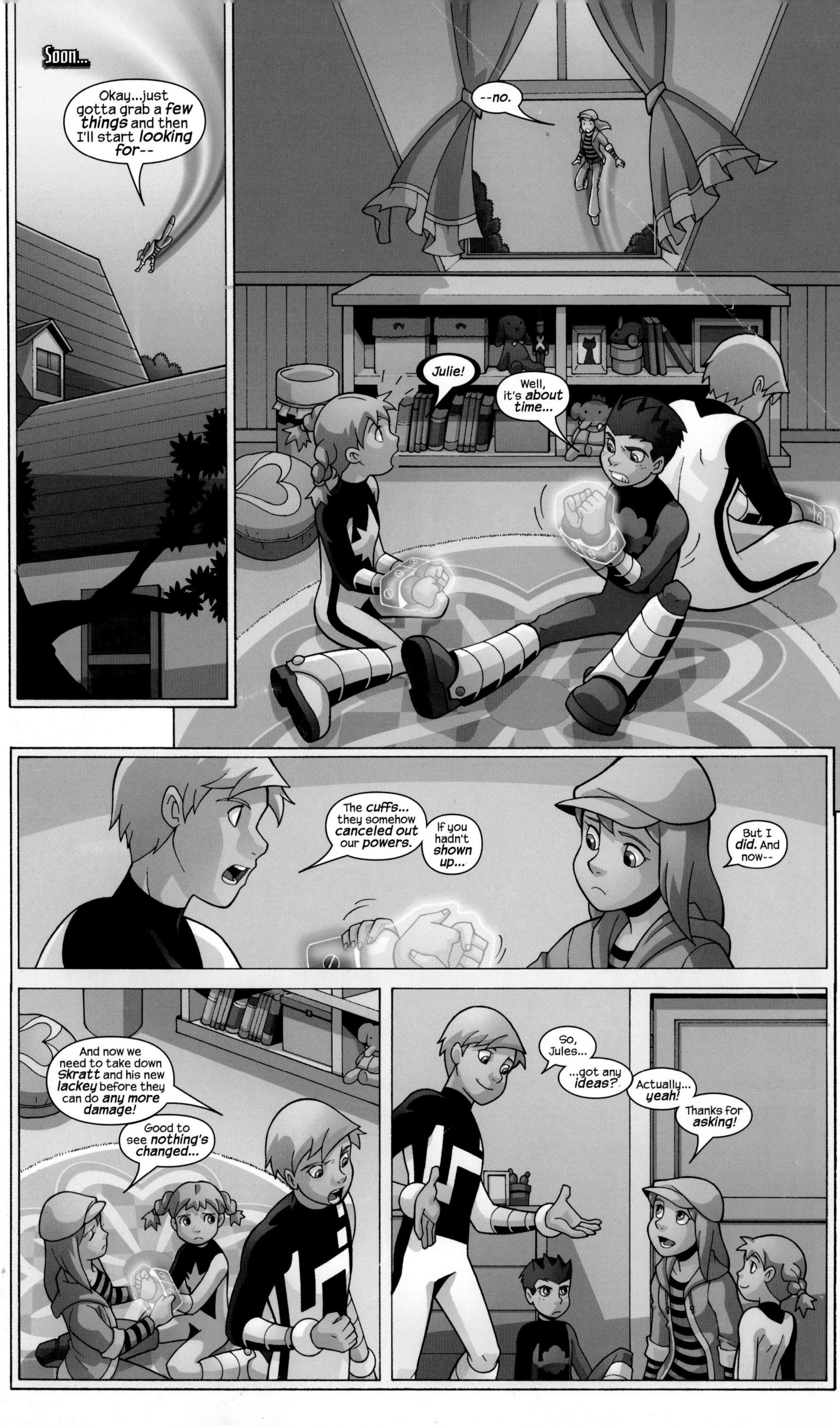
Soon...
Okay...just gotta grab a few things and then I'll start looking for--
--no.
Julie!
Well, it's about time...
The cuffs... they somehow canceled out our powers.
If you hadn't shown up...
But I did. And now--
And now we need to take down Skratt and his new lackey before they can do any more damage!
Good to see nothing's changed...
So, Jules...
...got any ideas?
Actually... yeah!
Thanks for asking!

You *sure* the *last kid* is gonna *show up*, Skratt?

She *must* return home *eventually...*

...and when she *does*, we'll--

You'll *what?*

The girl!

At last! She is *ours!*

Not yet, dino-breath!

TCHOOM!

First, you'll have to *catch* me!

Come back here!

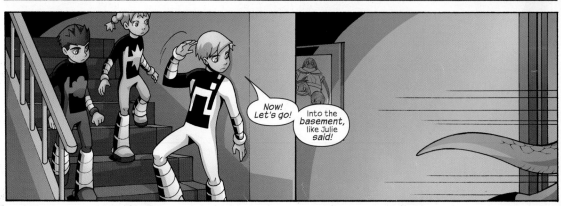

Now! Let's go!

Into the *basement*, like Julie said!

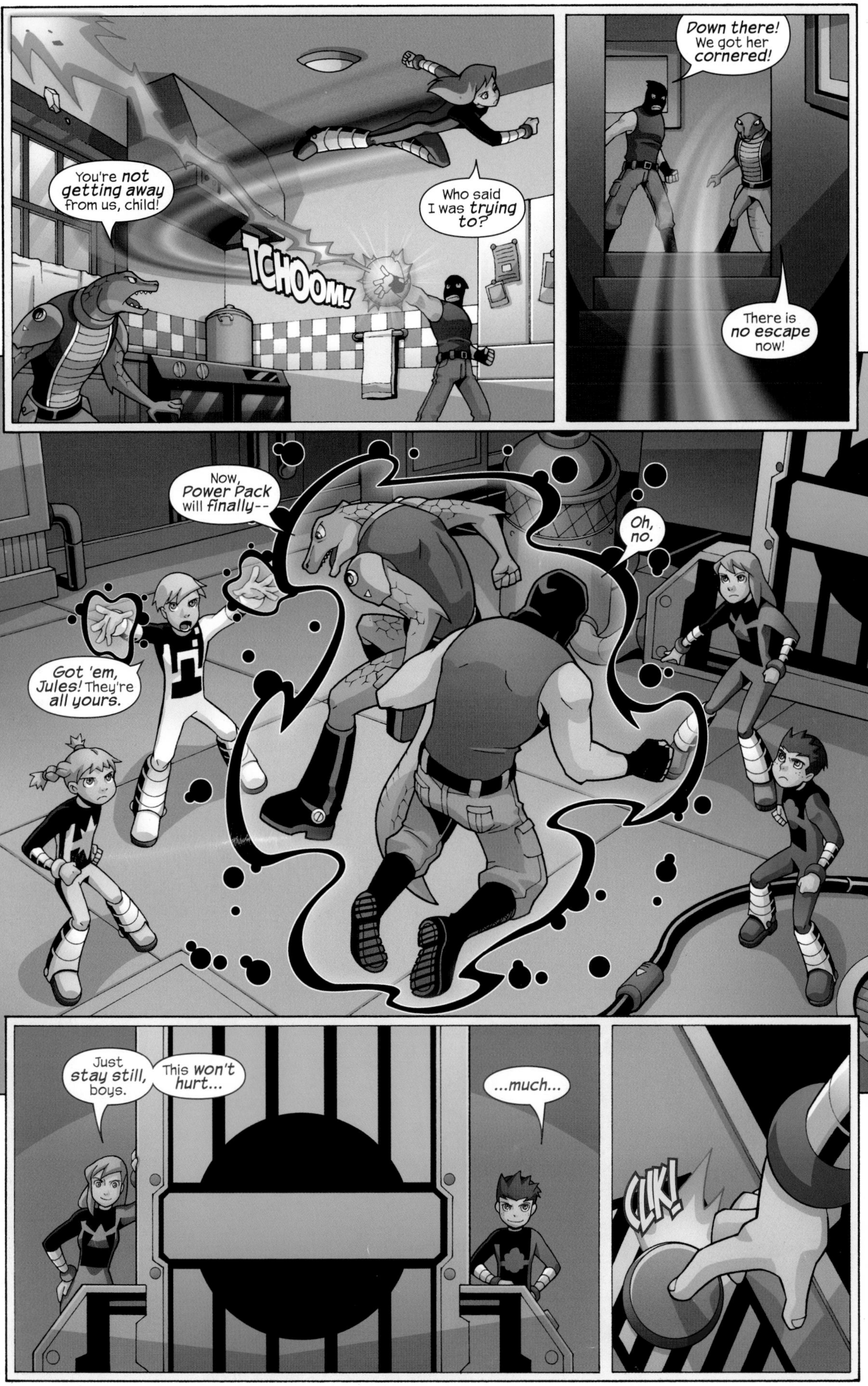
You're not getting away from us, child!
Who said I was trying to?
TCHOOM!
Down there! We got her cornered!
There is no escape now!
Now, Power Pack will finally--
Oh, no.
Got 'em, Jules! They're all yours.
Just stay still, boys.
This won't hurt...
...much...
CLIK!

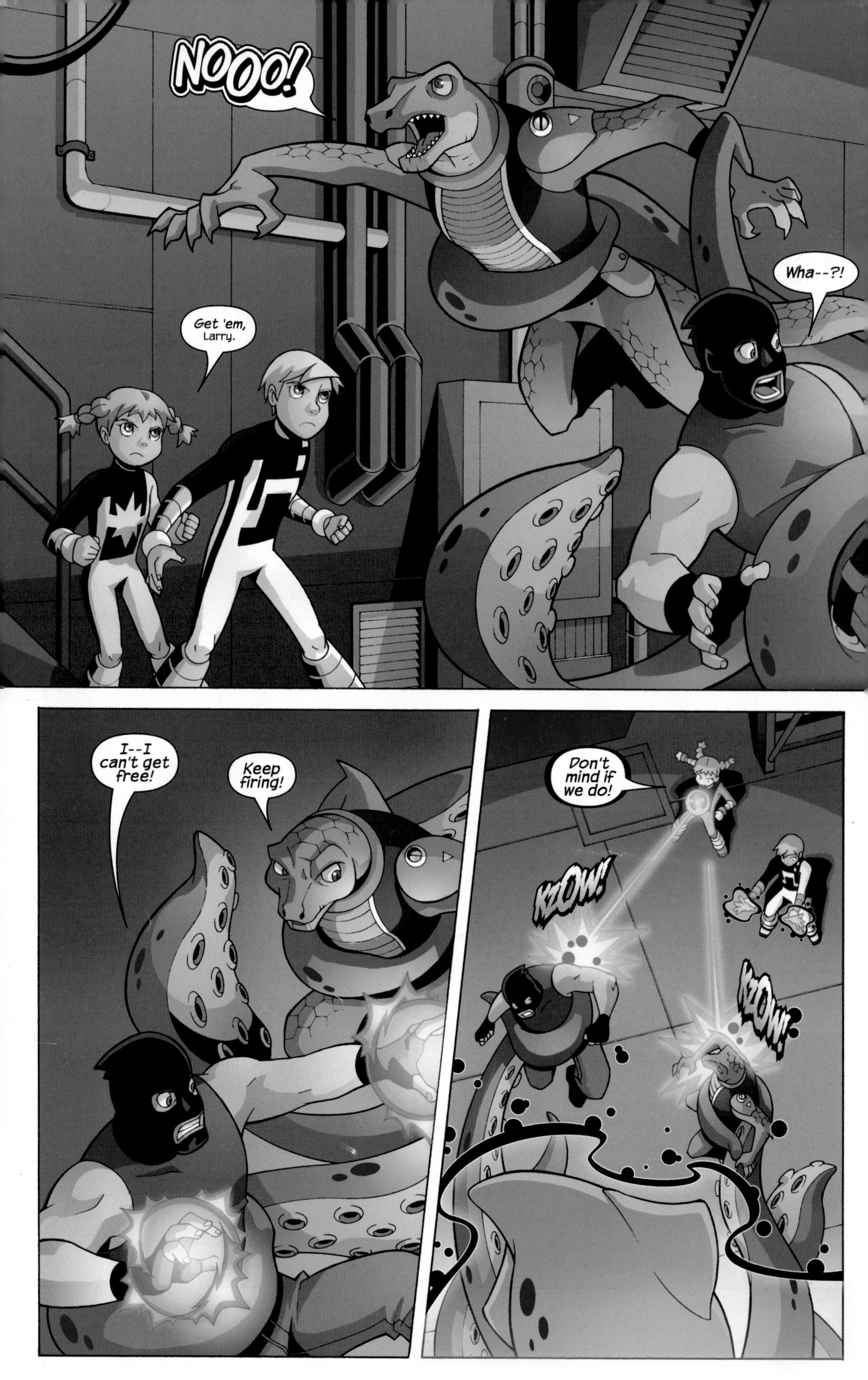
NOOO!
Get 'em, Larry.
Wha--?!
I--I can't get free!
Keep firing!
Don't mind if we do!
KZOW!
KZOW!

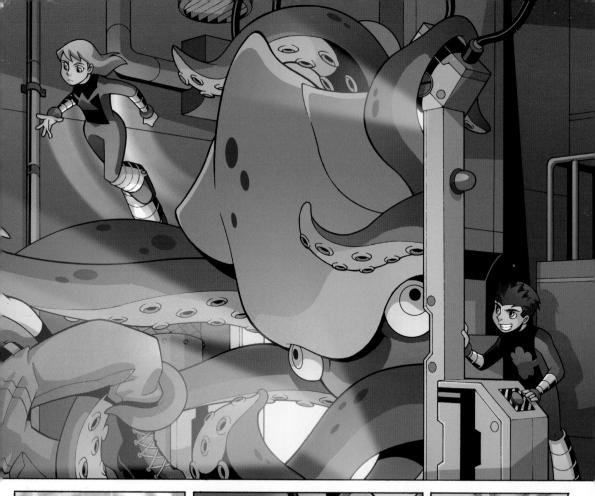

HEEELP!

They're through! Turn it off Jack!

Aye, aye, Captain...

KHWWWWW

Well...I think that's the *last* we'll be seeing of *them!*

Thank *goodness!* The less *bad guys* that know where we *live*, the *better!*

You *know*, maybe we oughta think about wearing *masks...*

Guys, I'm...I'm *really sorry* about all of this.

The *team*--the *family*-- it's real *important* to me.

I should *never* have tried to *walk away.*

We're sorry too, Julie.

You've *always* been a *valuable member* of Power Pack...

...but maybe we need to *remind* you of that *more often.*

Yeah, and I was *totally wrong* about your *powers.*

They really *are* good for something...

You *think so*, Jack?

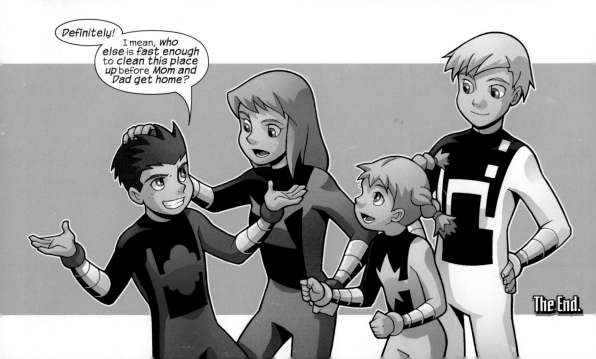

Definitely!

I mean, *who else* is *fast enough* to *clean this place up* before *Mom and Dad* get home?

The End.